**ReadZone Books Limited**

50 Godfrey Avenue
Twickenham
TW2 7PF
UK

*For Grandad with love – SM*

© ReadZone Books 2014
© in text Alan Durant 2007
© in illustrations Sue Mason 2007

First published in this edition by Evans Brothers Ltd, London in 2010.
Published in 2007 as *Froggy went a Hopping*

British Library Cataloguing in Publication Data (CIP) is available for this title.

Printed and bound in China for Imago

ISBN 978 1 78322 422 7

**Visit our website: www.readzonebooks.com**

# Hoppy Ever After!

by Alan Durant

illustrated by Sue Mason

It was a fine bright day and Froggy was feeling very hoppy.

His fingers itched and his webby toes twitched.

He wanted to leap and hop and spring and sing.

But Froggy was all alone and he wanted the whole world to share his hoppiness.

So Froggy hopped off his lily pad and out into the big wide world.

Froggy hop hop hopped until he came to some trees where birds were singing. Twitter, twitter, tweet, tweet!

Froggy's fingers itched and his webby toes twitched.

He was so very hoppy he just had to sing too.

Croak, croak, ribbit! Croak, croak, rib...

"Hey, frog!" a little bird voice piped. "You're ruining our song. Hop it!"

"Sorry," croaked Froggy and away he hopped.

Froggy hop hop hopped until he came to a meadow where bees swarmed in and out of flowers. Froggy's fingers itched and his webby toes twitched. He just had to join in. He poked his fingers into the flowers.

"Hey, that's our job, frog.
Leave those flowers alone!"
buzzed the bees angrily.
"Buzz off. Hop it!"

"Sorry," said Froggy and
away he hopped.

Froggy hop hop hopped to the top
of a hill where a band of bunnies was
jumping. Bounce, bounce, bounce!

Froggy's fingers itched and his webby
toes twitched.

He just had to bounce too.

But the bunnies were too fast and
soon they had all bounced away.
   Flop! Froggy was all alone ...
or was he?
   "Hey frog!" snarled a voice
behind him.
   Froggy turned to see...

A fox! An angry mean grumpy old fox.
"You just caused my lunch to vanish,"
said the fox.
"Sorry," gulped Froggy.
"Well," said the fox. "I guess today I'll
just have to eat frog instead."

Froggy's fingers quivered
and his webby toes shivered.
The fox pounced ...
and Froggy leapt.

Up up above the bunnies, the bees
and the birds, high high into the sky
leapt Froggy until ... flump!

Froggy's fingers itched and his webby toes twitched.
He wanted to twinkle too.

But he couldn't.
Poor Froggy. Tears plopped
from his big bulgy eyes.

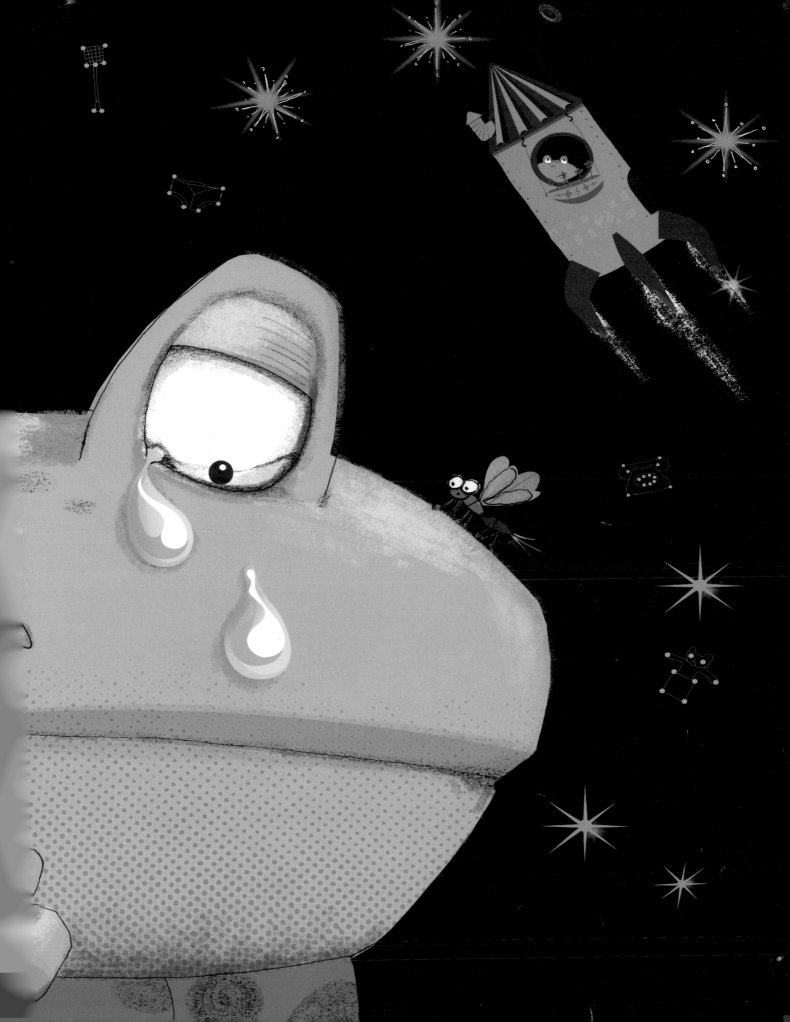

Suddenly thunder rumbled.
Lightning flashed.

Froggy's cloud turned black
and burst into raindrops.

Down
down
down fell Froggy down
down
down until ...

Splash! He landed back in his very own pond!

And there on his lily pad sat another frog.

"Hurrah!" cried the frog. "It's such a lovely wet night and I was feeling so hoppy. I wished for someone to share it with, and down you came like a falling star."

"Oh," said Froggy.

Froggy's fingers itched and his webby toes twitched.

How very very hoppy he was.

Then Froggy and his new friend hop
hop hopped together all night long and
lived hoppily ever after.